FOOD TRUCKS!

MARK TODD

HOUGHTON MIFFLIN HARCOURT

BOSTON NEW YORK

For Emmerson—Keep on truckin'!

www.hmhbooks.com

The text of this book is set in Humper and Zemke Hand. The illustrations are pen-and-ink and digitally colored.

Library of Congress Cataloging-in-Publication Data
Todd, Mark, 1970– author, illustrator.
Food trucks! / written and illustrated by Mark Todd.
      pp. c.m.
Summary: Uses illustrations and short rhymes, interspersed with facts about foods,
food related holidays, and more, to introduce food trucks and the many treats they offer,
from a full breakfast to a cupcake.
ISBN 978-0-544-15784-2
 [1. Stories in rhyme. 2. Street food—Fiction. 3. Food trucks—Fiction. 4. Trucks—Fiction.]
 I. Title.
PZ8.3.T562Foo 2014
[E]—dc23
2013018437

Manufactured in China
SCP 10 9 8 7 6 5 4 3 2 1
4500461156

HEY!

Here come the Food Trucks!
Talk about your meals on wheels.
These travelin' chow hounds
Are heading to your town . . .

Cookin' up a storm,
Revvin' up,
Takin' your order,
And servin' some tasty grub!

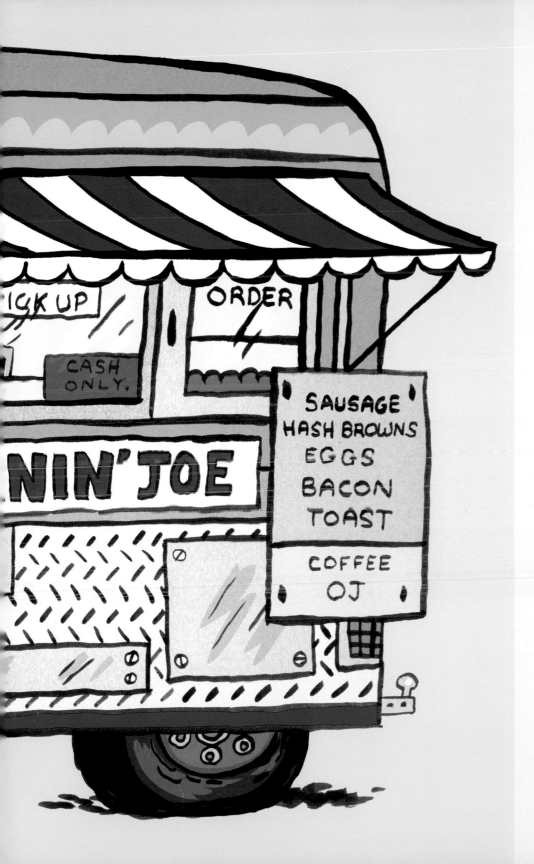

MORNIN' JOE
(BREAKFAST TRUCK)

Rise and shine!
Mornin's waitin',
Don't have time
For hesitatin'.

We'll head on down to grab a bite,
Then head off to the construction site.

Place your order,
Make it fast.
Time's a wastin'—
It's nearly past.

Order's up! I'm on my way
With just the thing to start my day!

Coffee, OJ, side of taters,
Scrambled egg—
See you later!

BETTER BURGER BUILDER BUS

(HAMBURGER TRUCK)

Wanna build a better burger?
Look no further
Than the Better Burger Builder Bus.

First you pick the perfect patty,
Put on some pickles,
Tomato, onions, and American cheese.
Add ketchup, mustard, and lettuce leaves.

We grill to perfection
Without exception—
We're the best Better Burger Builder
That's ever been.

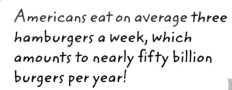

The world's largest burger weighed 2,014 pounds and was ten feet in diameter. Before it was topped with sixty pounds of bacon and forty pounds of cheese, it took a crane to flip the patty!

Americans eat on average three hamburgers a week, which amounts to nearly fifty billion burgers per year!

Some believe that a German man named Otto Kuase invented the hamburger when in 1891 he put a beef patty topped with a fried egg on a roll. The egg was soon dropped. He lived in Hamburg.

BUBBA Q
(BARBECUE TRUCK)

Head on down south—
Home to the banjo, country two-step,
And longhorn cattle steer.

Mosey on up for some barbecued brisket,
Sausage and slaw,
Okra, beans, and corn on the cob,

Rib-stickin',
Finger-lickin',
Toothpick-needin'—
This is some heavy eatin'.

From the Lone Star State of Texas
To the hills of Tennessee,
We serve up a generous portion
Of hospitality.

BRISKET: a cut of beef.

SLAW: (short for coleslaw) a salad consisting primarily of shredded raw cabbage combined with buttermilk and mayonnaise or sometimes vinegar and seasoning.

OKRA: a flowering plant that grows edible green seed pods, which are used in soups and stews or covered in a corn meal batter and fried.

Hailed as the world's largest BBQ on wheels, the Ultimate Smoker and Grill was forged from a converted eighteen-wheel semi-truck and can slow-smoke more than 2,000 pounds of meat and cook 1,000 hot dogs, 500 hamburgers, or 200 steaks.

May is National Barbecue Month (because you need more than a day).

In Texas, barbecue means beef, particularly brisket. But for most southerners, barbecue means pork.

THE PHARAOH'S TUMMY
(FALAFEL TRUCK)

Falafel—
Quite a mouthful—
Is made from chickpeas and wrapped in a pita.
A pita's a pocket that holds the falafel,
Which seems like a smart move to me.

If you want to keep the tongue loose,
Then try the couscous.
It complements the meal quite nicely.

FALAFEL: a ball or patty made of ground chickpeas and fried. It is believed to have originated in Egypt, where it was created to be eaten as a substitute for meat during Lent. Now it is enjoyed all over the Middle East and is a popular street food.

In 2012, ten chefs from Amman, Jordan, created the biggest falafel in the world—over 155 pounds. After the official weigh-in, the heavyweight was served up to more than six hundred people.

COUSCOUS: a coarsely ground pasta made from semolina, a type of wheat.

CHICKPEAS: also known as garbanzo beans, a member of the legume family.

PITA: flat, hollow unleavened bread that can be split open to hold a filling.

MR. COBB
(SALAD TRUCK)

For a healthy meal
With curb appeal,
Give this green machine a shot.

It's got shoots and roots and dried fruits,
Cucumbers, carrots, and croutons to boot,
Cheese and seeds and lots of leaves,
Including spinach, lettuce, kale, and
All sorts of yummy things.

Known as the "Salad Bowl of the World," Salinas Valley in California harvests much of the nation's lettuce, including iceberg, romaine, green leaf, red leaf, butter lettuce, and endive.

Recycled vegetable oil from the previous day's cooking powers some healthy eco-friendly trucks, and solar panels provide extra energy.

May is National Salad Month.

Green Truck in San Diego runs on vegetable oils, and all of their utensils are made out of potato starch so they are compostable.

There are two kinds of clam chowder popular today. Chowder with cream added is called New England chowder, while chowder with tomatoes added is called Manhattan chowder.

February 25 is National Clam Chowder Day.

The word clam is derived from the same Scottish word that means "vise" or "clamp."

PLEASE RECYCLE

CHARLEY CHOWDA

(CHOWDER TRUCK)

Nothing speaks louda
Than a bowl of clam chowda.

Clams, potatoes, onions, too—
Together make the hearty stew,
A tradition that we're very proud-a.

Fills you up,
Bowl or cup.
And don't forget the oyster crackers.

CHEDDAR CHUCK

(GRILLED CHEESE TRUCK)

This truck takes the cheese
And makes a melted masterpiece.

Grilled cheese?
Yes, please!

Provolone, Brie, or cheddar—
Nobody does it better!

Marvelously melted Monterey
Makes your heart simply melt away.

Pair it with soup
And, shoot, you've got a meal
That will make your day.

April is National Grilled Cheese Month.

SPRINKLES
(CUPCAKE TRUCK)

It's a piece of cake—
Though it doesn't take
Much time to eat one.

But make no mistake:
Too many cupcakes
Will surely bring

A bellyache.

The world record for eating cupcakes
was set by Pat Bertoletti, who
ate seventy-two cupcakes in
six minutes.

The world's largest cupcake was
four feet high and weighed more
than 1,000 pounds!

Cupcakes are thought to have
gotten their name because they
were originally baked in cups.

December 15 is National Cupcake Day.

Cupcakes are called fairy cakes in England and patty cakes in Australia.

TORO

(SUSHI TRUCK)

Have you ever tried sushi?
It has names like spider, rainbow, dragon, and philly:
Raw fish paired with rice,
Professionally sliced,
Pressed and hand rolled.
Works of art you can hold.

Or maybe the California roll?
Seaweed-wrapped crab, rice, cucumber, and avocado,
Made by a master chef aficionado.

If it's raw fish you're not quite sure of,
Then perhaps order the tempura.

Edamame,
Bright green soybeans in pods,
May seem a bit odd,
But believe me, they are quite tasty.

Originally, sushi arose out of a method of preserving food. Fish was placed in rice and allowed to ferment, which helped keep the fish edible.

A 489-pound bluefin tuna to be used for sushi was sold at Tokyo's Tsukiji Market for 155.4 million yen, or 1.8 million dollars.

June 18 is National Sushi Day in the United States. It is November 1 in Japan.

The Jogasaki truck in Los Angeles, California, is famous for their sushi burrito.

CURRY IN A HURRY
(INDIAN FOOD TRUCK)

From the land of spice
And basmati rice,
Where the elephant is most sacred,

Comes the most terrific of treats
Both savory and sweet
To enrich and enlighten your senses.

Try the samosa,
A pastry that most love,
Filled with onions, lentils, potatoes, and peas.

Or perhaps chicken tikka
Is what you seek—
A wonderful dish of flavor that surely will please.

A tandoori oven, a large clay pot with a hole in the top, is used to make naan bread and dishes such as tandoori chicken. Temperatures in the tandoor can reach 900 degrees!

CHICKEN TIKKA: small pieces of boneless chicken baked on skewers in a clay-based oven called a tandoor, after marinating in spices and yogurt. The word tikka means "bits or pieces."

Fragrant spices such as tumeric, coriander, cardamon, and cumin are used widely in Indian food, known for its intense aromas and unique flavors.

CURRY: vegetables and/or meat cooked with spices.

NAAN: a thick, flat bread baked in an oven.

EMPANADA: a pastry containing sweetened fillings such as pumpkin or sweet potato or savory fillings such as meat, cheese, and vegetables.

CARNITAS: roasted pork.

October 4 is National Taco Day.

CARNE ASADA: grilled beef.

HABAÑEROS: small, intensely hot chili peppers. They are short and squat with thin skin and are usually an orange or red color.

AMIGO
(TACO TRUCK)

What's up?
Surf's up!
Hang ten and then
Head on over to the taco truck!

Carne asada and empanadas
With rice and beans
Seems to really hit the spot!

Holy moly, guacamole!
How about a hot tamale?
Bean burrito or quesadilla?
We've got the whole enchilada.

Dare to add the habañero
If you like it REALLY hot!

DUTCH
(PRETZEL TRUCK)

Don't get tied up in knots
Or start to whine.
It's time to twist, shout, and dance about,
Unwind and intertwine—
Because it's all about the pretzel!

And wouldn't you know,
It's baked from dough:
Water, flour, and yeast.
Savory or sweet,
A unique knotlike treat.
Symmetrical.
Practical.
Overall,
Large or small,
It's what you call
A treat for all.

The world's largest pretzel, weighing 842 pounds and measuring nearly 27 feet in length, was made in Neufahm, Germany, in 2008.

National Pretzel Day is April 26.

Der Pretzel Wagen in Indianapolis, Indiana, is famous for their pretzel sliders.

The pretzel was invented in the seventh century by an Italian monk who decided to create a treat for his students. He rolled out ropes of dough, twisted them to resemble hands crossed on the chest in prayer, and baked them. He called them *pretiola*, Latin for "little reward."

Pretzels are believed to be the world's oldest snack.

In the seventeenth century, pretzels were known as "marriage knots" and signified oneness when eaten at weddings.

Thomas Jefferson, as legend has it, bought a waffle iron in France and began serving waffles in the White House, helping spark a fad for "waffle parties" nationwide.

Belgian waffles had their American debut at the Seattle World's Fair in 1962.

August 24 is National Waffle Day.

In Belgium, there are a number of different types of waffle, including the Brussels waffle, the Liège waffle, and the stroopwafel, though no waffles are known as a Belgian waffle.

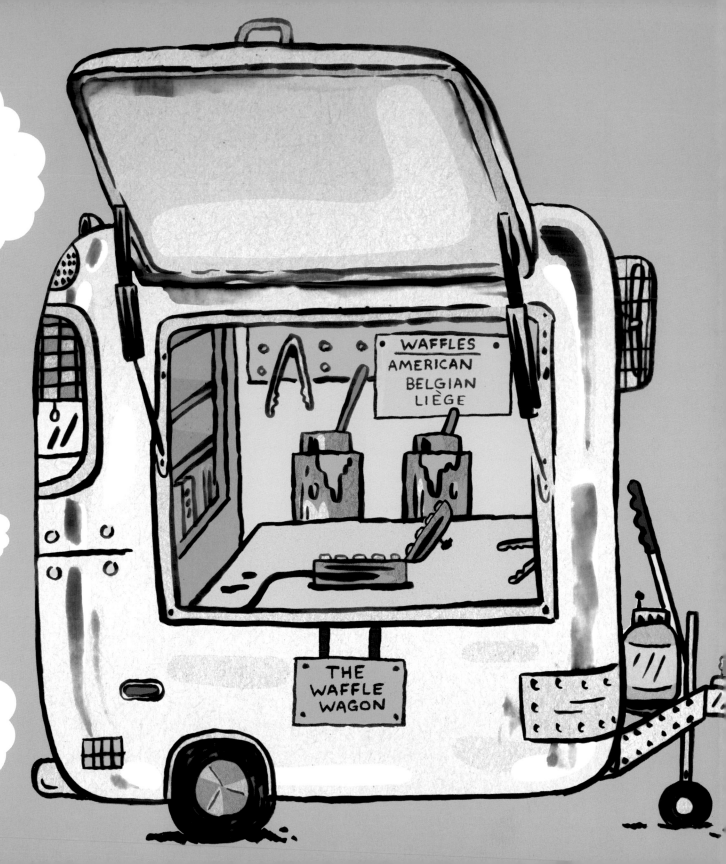

Since its opening in 1955, the Waffle House restaurant chain has served almost a billion waffles!

THE WAFFLE WAGON
(WAFFLE TRUCK)

It would be so awful,
A world without the waffle.

Breakfast would be a bore
If there was no syrup to pour
Or place a pat of butter onto.

I suppose the pancake would have to suffice,
Although, to me, it's not nearly as nice
As a waffle with those square pocket syrup holders.

Would it be so awful,
A world without the waffle?
Yes, I think it would.

The ice cream cone made its debut at the 1904 World's Fair in St. Louis, Missouri.

ICE QUEEN
(ICE CREAM TRUCK)

You're in luck!
The ice cream truck
Is heading to your neighborhood.

Ice cream cone,
Double dip,
Chocolate-sprinkled
Banana split!

You'll hear the tune
And very soon
Every kid will come running.

So grab a buck—
You're in luck!
The ice cream truck
Is heading down your street!

The average number of licks to finish off a single-scoop ice cream cone is fifty.

July is National Ice Cream Month.

Vanilla is the most popular flavor in the United States, followed by chocolate.

The Big Gay Ice Cream Truck in New York City serves cones with such toppings as wasabi pea dust, cayenne pepper, and pumpkin butter.

BRAIN FREEZE!
At least one-third of people experience it, and it isn't fun! Brain freeze happens when something cold touches the roof of your mouth, which stimulates a nerve center and causes the unpleasant sensation.

HEY!

There go the Food Trucks!
So long!
See you around,
Heading for another town.

They'll come back
And when they do
Be sure to order something new.